Contents

The Emperor's New Clothes

Retold from the original tale by Hans Christian Andersen

*T*HERE WAS ONCE an emperor who loved new clothes above everything else. Designers, tailors, clothmakers, dyers, and specialists in all sorts of needlework travelled to his city from all over the world. Anyone who could suggest flashy, fancy new outfits for the emperor was always very welcome at the palace.

One day, it was the turn of two weavers to be quickly ushered into the emperor's dressing room. The emperor, his

The Emperor's New Clothes

and other stories

Miles Kelly

First published in 2011 by Miles Kelly Publishing Ltd
Harding's Barn, Bardfield End Green, Thaxted, Essex, CM6 3PX, UK

2 4 6 8 10 9 7 5 3 1

Publishing Director Belinda Gallagher

Creative Director Jo Cowan

Editor Amanda Askew

Senior Designer Joe Jones

Production Manager Elizabeth Collins

Reprographics Anthony Cambray, Stephan Davis, Lorraine King, Jennifer Hunt

ISBN 978-1-84810-500-3

Printed in China

British Library Cataloguing-in-Publication Data
A catalogue record for this book is available from the British Library

ACKNOWLEDGEMENTS
Artworks are from the Miles Kelly Artwork Bank

Every effort has been made to acknowledge the source and copyright holder of each picture.
Miles Kelly Publishing apologises for any unintentional errors or omissions.

Made with paper from a sustainable forest

www.mileskelly.net
info@mileskelly.net

www.factsforprojects.com

butler and all his Officers of the Royal Wardrobe, gasped with amazement as they listened to them describe their work.

"We have created a special fabric that is so light and airy the wearer cannot feel it," the first weaver announced.

"Our samples are top secret, which is why we have not been able to bring any to show you," the second weaver explained.

"However we can assure you that not only are our designs and patterns exquisitely beautiful," said the first weaver, "but the fabric has the unique advantage that it is completely invisible to anyone not worthy of his job."

"Or who is just plain stupid!" laughed the second weaver, and the emperor and all his courtiers gasped and chuckled along.

"We would be honoured if you would like to order the first suit made out of this extraordinary fabric, your majesty," said the first weaver, bowing low.

The emperor clapped his hands with delight.

"I'd like to place an order right away!" he commanded, and he gave the two weavers a large sum of money so that they could buy the rare, expensive materials they needed and begin their work without delay.

The weavers set up their looms in the palace studio and got going right away. News of the strange cloth spread round the city like wildfire and soon everyone was talking about it. But the weavers worked behind closed doors and no one got even a glimpse of what they were doing. Still, day and night everyone heard the looms clicking and the shuttles flying, and work on the magical cloth seemed to be progressing well.

As the days went on, the emperor began to feel rather uneasy about seeing the cloth for the first time. 'Imagine if I can't see the fabric myself!' he thought to himself. 'How dreadfully embarrassing that would be!' The worried emperor decided to send his trusted old butler to see how the weavers were getting on. He was sure that his butler was both fit for his job and very wise, and would be sure to see the wonderful material.

The weavers bowed low and ushered the butler into the studio. But the butler couldn't see anything at all. Heavens above! the butler thought to himself. Those looms look totally bare to me! I must either be a bad butler, or else I'm an idiot. No one must find out...

So he praised the material that he could not see, told the king that the weavers' work was indeed magnificent, and everyone in the city heard that the cloth was truly unbelievable!

Soon afterwards, the weavers sent word to the emperor that they needed more money to buy essential items for the work. The emperor had been so delighted with the butler's report that he sent them twice as much money as before. The emperor was more excited than ever. "I'm going to have the most amazing suit of clothes in the world!" he giggled to himself.

Eventually, just as the impatient emperor thought he was going to explode with waiting, the weavers announced their work was finished. They went to the dressing room to present the material to the emperor amid fanfares of trumpets. "Is the cloth not beautiful beyond all imagining?" the weavers sighed.

The emperor smiled a wide smile, trying to hide his horror. All that the weavers appeared to be holding up before him was thin air. The emperor's worst fear had come true – to him the cloth was invisible! I cannot be thought to be a fool or not worthy to be ruler, the despairing emperor thought. So he beamed and leant forwards and inspected the air. "Wonderful! Splendid! Magnificent!" he cried, and his butler and all the Officers of the Royal Wardrobe nodded and cried out compliments. None of them could see anything either, but they weren't about to risk losing their jobs by admitting it.

So the weavers got out their tape measures and their scissors and they set about cutting the thin air (or so it seemed) into a pattern. All night long they sewed with needles that appeared to have no thread, and in the morning they announced that the emperor's new clothes were ready. "If your majesty would care to disrobe, we will dress you in the amazing garments."

The emperor swallowed hard and took off all his clothes. The weavers helped him on with the underpants and trousers and shirt and jacket that he couldn't see. "Aren't they lighter than cobwebs?" they sighed. The emperor spluttered his agreement. He couldn't feel that he had any clothes on at all.

The emperor stood back and looked at himself in the mirror. According to what he saw, he didn't have a stitch on! But he turned this way and that, pretending to admire himself. And the butler and all the Officers of the Royal Wardrobe cried out, "How wonderfully the new clothes fit you, sire!" and "We have never seen the like of the amazing colours!" and "The design is a work of genius!" – even though it looked to them as if the emperor was as naked as the day he was born.

Everyone else can see my new suit except me, the emperor thought to himself glumly. And he walked out of the palace to parade before the people in his marvellous new clothes.

The streets were lined with hundreds of people who ooohed! and aaaahed! over the emperor's invisible new clothes – for none of them wanted to admit that they couldn't see them.

Suddenly, a little boy's shrill voice rose over the applause of the crowd.

"But the emperor has nothing on!" the child shouted. "Nothing on at all!" Suddenly there was a stunned silence and the little boy found that hundreds of pairs of eyes were staring at him. Then someone sniggered… someone else tried to stifle a giggle… another person guffawed and snorted… and the whole crowd burst out into uncontrollable peals of laughter.

The emperor's face turned as red as a ripe tomato. "I am indeed a fool!" he murmured. "I have been swindled by two tricksters!" He ran back to the palace as fast as his short, naked legs could carry him – but the clever (and now very rich) weavers were long gone!

Rumpelstiltskin

Retold from the original tale
by the Brothers Grimm

ONCE UPON A TIME there was a miller. He was a foolish man who was always boasting. Then he went too far.

The king was riding past the mill with his huntsmen one day. The miller's daughter was sitting in the doorway, spinning. The king noticed that she was a pretty girl so he began talking to her. Her father came bustling up and began to tell the king what a splendid daughter she was.

"Why, your Majesty, she can even spin straw into gold!" boasted the ridiculous miller.

Needless to say, the poor girl could do nothing of the sort but the king thought this was an excellent way to refill the palace treasure house which was rather empty, so he took her back to the palace. He put her in a room with a great pile of straw and told her he wanted to see it all spun into gold the next morning, or else it would be the worse for her.

As soon as the door was locked she began to cry. The task was impossible. Then she heard a thin little voice.

"Do stop crying! You will make the straw all wet, and then we will have no chance of turning it into gold!"

There in front of her stood a strange little man. He had a tiny round body with long skinny legs and huge feet. His clothes looked as if they had seen better days, and on his head he wore a tall battered-looking hat.

"If you give me your necklace, I will do what the king has asked of you," he snapped.

The miller's daughter unclasped her necklace and handed it to the little man. He hid it deep in one of his pockets, and sat down by the spinning wheel.

The spinning wheel turned in a blur. The pile of straw grew smaller, and the mound of shining gold grew higher. As the first light of day shone in through the window it was all done.

The strange little man disappeared as suddenly as he had appeared. The king was delighted with the great pile of gold, and asked the miller's daughter to marry him. She was too shy to reply so the king just took her silence as her agreement and married her anyway that afternoon.

For a while all was well. But then the treasure house grew empty again so once more the poor girl, now the queen, was locked in a room with a pile of straw and a spinning wheel.

As the queen wept, once more the strange little man appeared. The queen asked him to help her again, and offered him all the rich jewels she was wearing. But the strange little man was not interested in jewels.

"You must promise to give me your first born child," he whispered.

The queen was desperate. But she promised and the little man sat down at the spinning wheel. A great pile of gold appeared by the side of the spinning wheel, and by dawn the straw had all gone. The king was delighted and for a while all was well. Then the queen gave birth to a beautiful baby, and she remembered with dread her promise to the strange little man. Seven days after the baby was born, he appeared by the side of the cradle. The queen wept.

"There you go again," said the little man crossly, "always crying!"

"I will do anything but let you have my baby," cried the queen.

"Very well then, anything to make you stop crying,"

said the little man, who by now was dripping wet from all the queen's tears. "If you can guess my name in three days, I will let you keep your baby," he said and disappeared as suddenly as he had appeared.

The next morning the little man appeared by the side of the cradle. The queen had sent messengers out far and wide to see if anyone knew the strange little man's name.

"Is it Lacelegs?" she asked.

"No!"

"Is it Wimbleshanks?"

"No!"

"Is it Bandyknees?"

"No!"

And the little man disappeared as suddenly as he had appeared. The queen sent out even more messengers to the lands far beyond the borders of the kingdom. The second morning the strange little man appeared by the side of the cradle.

"Is it Bluenose?" the queen asked.

"No!"

"Is it Longtooth?"

"No!"

"Is it Skinnyribs?"

"No!" and the little man disappeared with a nasty laugh.

The queen waited up all night as her messengers came in one by one, and just as she was giving up all hope of saving her precious baby, in came the very last one. He was utterly exhausted but he brought the queen the best of news. In a deep, deep, dark forest he had found a strange little man dancing round a fire, singing this song.

"Today I brew, today I bake,

Tomorrow I will the baby take.

The queen will lose the game,

Rumpelstiltskin is my name!"

When the strange little man appeared again by the cradle, the queen pretended she still did not know his name.

"Is it Gingerteeth?" she asked.

"No!" said the little man, and he picked the baby up.

"Is is Silverhair?" asked the queen.

"No!" said the little man, and he started to walk towards the door, with a wicked smile.

"Is it Rumpelstiltskin?" asked the queen, and she ran up to the strange little man.

"Some witch told you that!" shrieked the little man, and he stamped his foot so hard that he fell through the floor and was never seen again. The queen told the king the whole story and he was so pleased his baby and his queen were safe that he forgot to be cross with the miller who had told such a terrible fib in the first place!

Snow White and the Seven Dwarfs

Retold from the original tale
by the Brothers Grimm

THE QUEEN WAS sitting at the window sewing, and thinking about her baby who would be born soon. As she sewed she pricked her finger, and red blood fell on the snow by the ebony window ledge.

"I wish that my daughter be as white as snow, as black as ebony and as red as blood," she said to herself, and so it happened. Her tiny daughter had snow-white skin, lips as red as blood and hair as black as ebony, so she was called Snow White. But the queen died and the king married again. His new wife was very beautiful but she had a cold heart, and she did not love Snow White.

Every morning the new queen would look into her magic mirror and say,

"Mirror, mirror on the wall
Who is fairest in the land?"
and the mirror would always reply, "Thou, oh queen, Thou art fairest in the land."

So the queen was content. Seven years passed and Snow White grew into a lovely young girl, with her mother's gentle nature.

One morning the queen looked into her mirror as usual, but the mirror's reply filled her with a deep envy.

"Thou, oh queen, Thou art indeed fair

But Snow White is the fairest in the land."

She ordered her woodsman to kill Snow White. But he could not bear to do such a wicked deed so he hid Snow White deep in the forest. Poor Snow White wandered about until she was utterly weary.

Suddenly, she caught sight of a light through the trees in the distance. It came from a little house with a lantern glowing in one small window. The door swung open at her touch, so she stepped inside. Everything was as neat as a new pin. A scrubbed wooden table was set, with seven plates and seven cups. Seven little chairs were ranged round the table, and along the back wall there were seven little beds, each with a brightly coloured blanket.

There was a basket of logs beside the fireplace, and Snow White soon had a cheerful fire going. She sat in one of the little chairs and before long was fast asleep.

Now the cottage belonged to seven dwarfs and when they came home that evening, they were very worried to discover Snow White fast asleep. They tiptoed round preparing their supper, but as the wonderful smell of stew filled the room, Snow White awoke with a start. She was very surprised to see seven little faces looking at her, but soon she was telling them how she came to be in the forest. They were very angry when they heard about the wicked queen.

"Might I stay with you?" asked Snow White. "I could look after you, and have supper ready every night."

The dwarfs were just delighted with this suggestion, and immediately set about making Snow White her own chair by the fireside and her own bed.

Back in the castle, the queen looked into her mirror in the morning, and asked,

"Mirror, mirror on the wall,

Who is fairest in the land?"

But you can imagine her rage when the mirror replied,

"Thou, oh queen, Thou art indeed fair,

But Snow White with the seven dwarfs does dwell

and she is fairest in the land."

So the wicked queen disguised herself as an old pedlar, and searched out the dwarfs' cottage. Snow White did not recognize the queen.

"Goodness me, you need new laces for your dress," said the old woman, and she pulled the new laces so tightly that Snow White was unable to breathe.

When the dwarfs came home that evening, they were horrified to discover Snow White lying on the floor as if dead. They lifted her up and, of course, saw the laces. They quickly cut the tight cord and the colour came back to Snow White's cheeks.

"Now you know the queen will stop at nothing," they

cried. "You must not let anyone indoors again."

The queen looked in her mirror the next morning, and went white with rage when it told her Snow White was still the fairest in the land. She disguised herself as a gypsy, selling wooden pegs and combs. Snow White remembered what the dwarfs had said and would not open the door. But the gypsy passed one of the combs through the window, and the minute it touched her hair, Snow White fell down in a faint for the comb was poisoned.

When the dwarfs came home and found Snow White, they immediately suspected the queen. They found the comb and pulled it out, and Snow White sat up, quite recovered. They pleaded with her to be more careful the next morning when they set off for work.

So when a farmer's wife appeared trying to sell apples, Snow White would not even open the window.

"Why, anyone would think I was trying to poison you," said the farmer's wife, who was, of course, the wicked queen in disguise.

"I only want to give you some apples. Look how juicy they are!" and she took a big bite out of one.

So Snow White thought it must be all right and she took the apple. But the queen had poisoned it on one side only, and the minute Snow White took a bite she fell down dead.

This time when the dwarfs came home, there was nothing they could do. Snow White was indeed dead. They could not bear to bury her in the cold earth so they placed her in a glass coffin. They wrote her name on the side in silver and put the coffin in a sheltered part of the forest, and planted wild flowers all round about.

When the queen looked into her mirror the next morning, it gave her the answer she wanted.

"Thou, oh queen,
Thou art fairest in the land."

Years and years passed. Snow White lay in her coffin, looking as beautiful as ever. The dwarfs watched over her day and night, and one day they found a young prince kneeling by the side of the glass coffin. He had fallen in love with Snow White the moment he had set eyes on her. When the dwarfs saw how deeply the prince felt about their beloved Snow White, they agreed that he take the glass coffin to his palace where he wished to set it in his rose gardens.

As the prince lifted the glass coffin, the piece of poisoned apple flew from her lips, and Snow White opened her eyes. She saw the prince, she saw her faithful dwarfs and she cried, "Where am I? What has happened?"

There was huge excitement as everyone tried to talk at once. The prince wasted no time and asked Snow White to marry him. She agreed as long as the dwarfs could come and live at the palace as well, and they all lived happily ever after.

But what of the queen? She looked in her mirror the morning Snow White and the prince were to be married.

"Mirror, mirror on the wall
Who is fairest in the land?"
The mirror replied,
"Snow White, oh queen,
Snow White who marries her prince today,
She is fairest in the land."

The queen was so ugly in her rage that the mirror cracked from side to side. And she was never able to look in a mirror ever again as long as she lived.

The Little Mermaid

Retold from the original tale by
Hans Christian Andersen

FAR, FAR OUT in the ocean, the water is as blue as cornflowers and deeper than the tallest mountain. It is there that the sea-people live, and in the very deepest waters lies the Sea King's palace of coral and mother-of-pearl. The Sea King's beloved wife had died, so his mother, the old queen, took care of his six beautiful mermaid daughters. All day long, the princesses sang and danced, swimming in and out of the pillars and halls of the palace. Sometimes shy, brightly coloured fish swam up to eat out of their hands. And at other times, each would tend the little garden that she cared for in the royal grounds. Each mermaid princess gave her garden its own particular style and design: one was shaped like a whale; another had a rockery of shells; yet another had flowerbeds where the sea-horses came to graze. But the youngest mermaid's garden was shaped like the sun that shone on the world above the sea, and the flowers that grew there blazed red and orange and yellow like the sunlight.

The little mermaid had never been up to the ocean's surface and seen the upper world, for the princesses were only allowed to do so when they reached fifteen years old. But the little mermaid longed for that day to come. She loved to hear the stories her grandmother told of people and ships and cities and animals and meadows and forests and the like. And many a night the little mermaid stood at her open chamber window, peering up at the watery reflections of the moon and the stars and the dark shapes of ships as they passed like clouds above her.

When each of her sisters came of age, the little mermaid begged them eagerly to tell her everything they had seen. Then at last, she turned fifteen and it was her turn to see the upper world for herself.

The little mermaid thought it was more beautiful than she had ever imagined. Her head broke through the foam when the sun had just gone down and the clouds looked as if they were on fire with red and gold. The sound of music and singing was coming from a tall-masted ship bedecked all about with coloured flags and banners. Suddenly rockets zoomed up from it into the sky which exploded into stars that fell glittering all around her – the little mermaid had never seen fireworks before. When she was lifted up on the swell of the sea, she saw onto the ship's magnificent deck and understood the reason for the wonderful celebrations: it was the birthday party of a prince, more handsome than any merman she had ever seen.

As the little mermaid gazed with delight at the prince and his ship, she heard a familiar rumbling stirring deep within the sea. A storm was coming! All at once the sky darkened. Sheets of rain lashed the ship. The waves towered into mountains that hurled the ship upwards and sent it crashing down towards the depths. The little mermaid saw with alarm that the ship wouldn't be able to hold out against the might of the weather and the ocean, and she ducked under the waves as wooden planks and other pieces of the ship came flying out of the darkness at her head. Through the murky waters, the little mermaid was horrified to see human bodies come floating down around her – and among them was her beautiful prince, choking and gasping for air.

The little mermaid shot through the water and clutched him close to her, and began swimming up to the light until his head was above water. The little mermaid hauled the exhausted prince to the shore and let the waves wash him onto the sand, and she stayed in the foam and watched him until the storm had died away and the morning sunlight came streaming warmly through the clouds. Then she saw the green hills for the first time and heard the peal of bells, and she saw a group of young girls come skipping out of a white building with a cross on the top. One of the girls noticed the prince where he lay. She ran to him and laid his head in her lap, and slowly the prince opened his eyes. He looked up at the girl and smiled, and the little mermaid turned away sadly, for she knew the prince thought it was that girl who had rescued him.

From that moment on, the little mermaid was thoughtful and sad. She longed to see her handsome prince again, to tell him that she loved him and wanted to be with him forever. She wanted to be human more than anything else in the whole world. There was only one thing she could do: make the dangerous journey to the cold, dark depths of the ocean to see the Water-Witch.

The Water-Witch's lair was set about with the skeletons of humans she had drowned and the remains of ships she had wrecked. The little mermaid trembled with fear as she explained why she had come.

"What you long for is extremely difficult to give," the Water-Witch cackled.

"I can make your tail disappear and give you legs so that you can walk about with the humans in the world above. But every step you take will be as painful as if you are treading on knives. And I cannot make your prince fall in love with you. It is up to you, and you alone, to do that. If your prince marries another, the morning afterwards your heart will break and you will turn to foam on the water."

The little mermaid shuddered, but she bade the Water-Witch continue.

"The price for such strong magic is very high," spat the witch. "Once I have given you legs, there is no changing your mind. You will never be able to return to the sea as a mermaid to see your family... And there is one more thing. I cannot mix the potion you need unless you give me your voice."

The little mermaid longed for her prince and for a human soul that she whispered, "So be it." The words were the last sounds she ever uttered. For then the Water-Witch took the little mermaid's voice and brewed up an evil-smelling potion for her in exchange.

The little mermaid felt as if her heart would break

with grief as she swam back past her father's palace, leaving her sleeping family for the world above. She splashed onto the sand, half-choking through her tears and half-gasping for air, and looked at her beautiful silvery fishtail for the last time. Then the little mermaid raised the witch's brew to her lips and drank deeply. At once pain wracked her body and she fell into a dead faint…

The little mermaid awoke to find her handsome prince standing over her, looking worried. "Are you all right?" he asked, but the little mermaid couldn't reply. Instead, she smiled as she looked down at her body and saw that she had the prettiest pair of legs she could have wished for. Falteringly, she stood up for the very first time. The little mermaid put out her foot – and it was true, each step was like treading on knives. But soon she was dancing and running and skipping along the beach for joy, and the prince was utterly enchanted.

The prince took his new little friend back to the palace and dressed her in fine robes of silk and satin. He didn't seem to mind that she was dumb, and kept her by his side at all times, calling her "my beautiful little foundling".

Yet although the little mermaid was happier than she

had ever dreamed was possible, there was a sadness in her eyes and a heaviness in her heart. Each night, she would creep out of the palace and go down to the seashore. Sometimes she saw her sisters way out among the surf, and they would sing to her sadly as they floated on the waves. Once, she even thought she glimpsed the golden crowns of her father and grandmother – but perhaps it was just the moonlight glinting on the water.

Eventually a day came when the prince led the little mermaid onto a fine ship just like the one from which she had rescued him. They sailed for a night and a day, and all the time the little mermaid longed to leap into the waves and dive down to see her family. The ship finally arrived in the harbour of a neighbouring kingdom, and the people lined the streets to meet them, cheering. "See how they welcome me," the prince whispered to the little mermaid. "For today I am going to marry their princess."

The little mermaid felt as if someone had grabbed

her heart with icy fingers. Surely it couldn't be true? But when the prince's bride came running down the palace steps to meet him, the little mermaid understood. It was the girl who had found him on the beach; the girl whom the prince thought had saved him from the sea; the girl whom the prince thought was the little mermaid.

That afternoon, the little mermaid stood in church dressed in silk and gold, holding the bride's train. And all the way back to the ship, she cried silent, dry tears.

That night, as the splendid ship floated on the waves, there were flags and fireworks and music and dancing – and the little mermaid felt no more a part of the celebrations than she had when she had watched the prince's birthday party from afar.

The little mermaid stood on the deck all night and listened to the sighing of the sea. She felt the warm night wind on her face and her hair floated in the damp sea mists. When the first rays of the dawn lit up the horizon, the little mermaid prepared herself to dissolve into foam on the waves. But instead, she saw transparent beings of light flying to her through the air. They lifted her up on their wings and soared off into

the sky, and the little mermaid found that she was one of them. "We are the daughters of the air. We do not have an immortal soul, but if we perform enough acts of goodness, we will win one for ourselves. And this is your reward for the suffering you have endured."

The little mermaid raised her hands towards the sun and the tears in her eyes were tears of joy. She looked down upon the prince and his bride on their ship. They were searching for her in the water, thinking she had fallen overboard. But the little mermaid didn't stay to watch them for long. She blew them a kiss and flew onwards with the daughters of the air.